This edition published by Parragon in 2013
Parragon
Chartist House
15-17 Trim Street
Bath BA1 1HA, UK
www.parragon.com

Illustrated by Chameleon Designs, Daniel Howarth, Paula Martyr, Anna Leplar, Claire
Mumford, Chris Forsey, Diana Catchpole, Robin Edmonds and Jo Brown.
Pink Princess by Lulu Frost   Illustrated by Fran Brylewska and Lorna Brown
Edited by Robyn Newton   Production by Jon Wakeham

ISBN 978-1-4723-1607-3

Printed in China

My
Princess
purse

PaRRagon

Bath · New York · Singapore · Hong Kong · Cologne · Delhi
Melbourne · Amsterdam · Johannesburg · Shenzhen

This book belongs to:

....

....

Contents

Snow White

Long, long ago, in a faraway land, there lived a king and queen who had a beautiful baby girl. Her lips were as red as cherries, her hair was as black as coal, and her skin was as white as snow – her name was Snow White.

Sadly, the queen died and years later the king married again. The new queen was very beautiful, but also evil, cruel and vain.

She had a magic
mirror, and every day
she looked into it
and asked, "Mirror,
mirror on the wall,
who is the fairest
one of all?"

And every day,
the mirror replied,
"You, O Queen, are
the fairest!"

Time passed, and every year Snow White grew more beautiful. The queen became increasingly jealous of her stepdaughter.

One day, the magic mirror gave the queen a different answer to her question. "Snow White is the fairest one of all!" it replied.

The queen was furious. She ordered her huntsman to take Snow White deep into the forest and kill her.

But the huntsman couldn't bear to harm Snow White. "Run away!" he told her. "Run away and never come back, or the queen will kill us both!" Snow White fled deep into the forest.

As Snow White rushed through the trees she came upon a tiny cottage. She knocked at the door and then went in – the house was empty. There she found a tiny table with seven tiny chairs. Upstairs there were seven little beds. Exhausted, she lay down across them and fell asleep.

Many hours later, Snow White woke to see seven little faces peering at her. The dwarfs, who worked in a diamond mine, had returned home and wanted to know who the pretty young girl was.

Snow White told them her story and why she had to run away. They all sat round and listened to her tale.

11

When she had finished, the eldest dwarf said, "If you will look after our house for us, we will keep you safe. But please don't let anyone into the cottage while we are at work!"

The next morning, when the wicked queen asked the mirror her usual question, she was horrified when it answered, "The fairest is Snow White, gentle and good. She lives in a cottage, deep in the wood!"

The queen turned green with rage; she had been tricked. She magically disguised herself as an old pedlar and set off into the wood to seek out Snow White and kill the girl herself.

That afternoon, Snow White heard a tap-tapping at the window. She looked out and saw an old woman with a basket full of bright ribbons and laces.

12

"Pretty things for sale," cackled the old woman.

Snow White remembered the dwarfs' warning. But the ribbons and laces were so lovely, and the woman seemed so harmless, that she let her in.

"Try this new lace in your dress, my dear," said the old woman. Snow White was thrilled and let the lady thread the laces into her bodice. But she pulled them so tight that Snow White fainted.

Certain that at last she had killed her stepdaughter, the queen raced through the forest, back to her castle, laughing evilly.

That evening, the dwarfs returned home. They were shocked to discover Snow White lying on the floor - lifeless. They loosened the laces on her dress so she could breathe and made her promise once again not to let any strangers in when they were at work.

The next day, when the mirror told the queen that Snow White was still alive, she was livid and vowed to kill her once and for all. She disguised herself and went back to the cottage.

This time the old woman took with her a basket of lovely red apples. She had poisoned the biggest, reddest one of all. She knocked on the door and called out, "Juicy red apples for sale."

The apples looked so delicious that Snow White just had to buy one. She opened the door and let the old woman in.

"Oh my, what pretty, rosy cheeks you have, deary," said the woman, "the very colour of my apples. Here, take a bite and see how good they are." She handed Snow White the biggest one...

Snow White took a large bite and fell to the floor, dead. The old woman fled into the forest, happy at last.

15

This time, the dwarfs could not bring Snow White back to life.

Overcome with grief, they placed her gently in a glass coffin and carried it to a quiet clearing in the forest. And there they sat, keeping watch over their beloved Snow White.

One day, a handsome young prince came riding through the forest and saw the beautiful young girl in the glass coffin. He fell in love with her at once and begged the dwarfs to let him take her back to his castle.

At first the dwarfs refused, but when they saw how much the prince loved their Snow White, they agreed.

As the prince lifted the coffin to carry it away, he stumbled, and the piece of poisoned apple fell from Snow White's mouth, where it had been lodged all this time. Snow White's eyes fluttered open, and she looked up and saw the handsome young man.

"Where am I?" she asked him in a bewildered voice. "Who are you?"

"I am your prince," he said. "And you are safe with me now. Please will you marry me and come to live in my castle?" He leant forward and kissed her cheek.

"Oh, yes, sweet prince," cried Snow White. "Of course I will."

The next day, the magic mirror told the wicked queen of Snow White's good fortune. She flew into a rage and disappeared in a flash of lightning.

Snow White married her prince, and went to live in his castle. The seven dwarfs visited them often, and Snow White and her prince lived happily ever after.

The Frog Prince

There was once a king who had but one
daughter. Being his only child, she wanted for
nothing. She had a nursery full of toys, a pony to
ride and a wardrobe bursting with pretty dresses.
But, for all this, the princess was lonely.
"How I wish I had someone to play with,"
she sighed.

The princess's favourite toy was a beautiful golden ball. Every day she would play with her ball in the palace garden. When she threw the ball up in the air, it seemed to take off of its own accord and touch the clouds before landing in the princess's hands again.

One windy day the princess was playing in the garden as usual. She threw her golden ball high into the air, but instead of returning to her hands, the wind blew the ball into the fishpond. The princess ran to the pond, but to her dismay the ball had sunk right to the bottom. "Whatever shall I do?" wailed the girl. "Now I have lost my favourite toy." And she sat down beside the pond and cried.

All at once she heard a loud PLOP! and a large green frog landed on the grass beside her. "Eeeuugh! Go away, you nasty thing!" screamed the princess.

To her astonishment, the frog spoke to her. "I heard you crying," he said in a gentle voice, "and I wondered what the matter was. Can I help you in any way?"

"Why, yes!" exclaimed the princess, once she had got over the shock of being addressed by a frog. "My ball has sunk to the bottom of the pond. Would you fish it out for me?"

"Of course I will," replied the frog. "But in return, what will you give me?"

"You can have my jewels, my finest clothes and even my crown if you will find my ball," said the princess hastily, for she was truly eager to get her favourite toy back.

"I do not want your jewels, your clothes or your crown," replied the frog. "I would like to be your friend. I want to return with you to the palace and eat from your golden plate and sip from your golden cup. At night I want to sleep on a cushion made of silk next to your bed and I want you to kiss me goodnight before I go to sleep."

"I promise all you ask," said the girl, "if only you will find my golden ball."

"Remember what you have promised," said the frog, as he dived deep into the pond. At last he surfaced again with the ball and threw it onto the grass beside the princess. She was so overjoyed she forgot all about thanking the frog – let alone her promise – and ran all the way back to the palace.

That evening the king, the queen and the princess were having dinner in the great hall of the palace, when a courtier approached the king and said, "Your majesty, there is a frog at the door who says the princess has promised to share her dinner with him."

"Is this true?" demanded the king, turning to the princess and looking rather angry.

"Yes, it is," said the princess in a small voice. And she told her father the whole story.

"When a promise is made it must be kept, my girl," said the king. "You must ask the frog to dine with you."

Presently, the frog hopped into the great hall and round to where the princess was sitting. With a great leap he was up on the table beside her. She stifled a scream.

"You promised to let me eat from your golden plate," said the frog, tucking into the princess's food. The princess felt quite sick and pushed the plate away from her. Then to her horror the frog dipped his long tongue into her golden cup and drank every drop. "It's what you promised," he reminded her.

When he had finished, the frog stretched his long, green limbs, yawned and said, "Now I feel quite sleepy. Please take me to your room."

"Do I have to?" the princess pleaded with her father.

"Yes, you do," said the king sternly. "The frog helped you when you were in need and you made him a promise."

So the princess carried the frog to her bedroom, but as they reached the door she said, "My bedroom's very warm. I'm sure you'd be more comfortable out here where it's cool."

But as she opened the bedroom door, the frog leapt from her hand and landed on her bed.

"You promised that I could sleep on a silk cushion next to your bed," said the frog.

"Yes, yes, of course," said the princess, looking with horror at the froggy footprints on her clean, white sheets.

She called to her maid to bring a cushion.

The frog jumped onto the cushion and looked as though he was going to sleep.

"Good," thought the princess, "he's forgotten about my final promise."

But just as she was about to get into bed, he opened his eyes and said, "What about my goodnight kiss?"

"Oh, woe is me," thought the princess as she closed her eyes and pursed her lips towards the frog's cold and clammy face and kissed him.

"Open your eyes," said a voice that didn't sound a bit like the frog's. She opened her eyes and there, standing before her, was a prince. The princess stood there in dumbstruck amazement.

"Thank you," said the prince. "You have broken a spell cast upon me by a wicked witch. She turned me into a frog and said the spell would only be broken if a princess would eat with me, sleep beside me and kiss me."

28

They ran to tell the king what had happened. He was delighted and said, "You may live in the palace from now on, for my daughter needs a friend."

And indeed, the prince and princess became the best of friends and she was never lonely again. He taught her to play football with the golden ball and she taught him to ride her pony. One day, many years later, they were married and had lots of children. And, do you know, their children were particularly good at leapfrog.

The Enchanted Garden

Princess Sylvie grew up in a beautiful castle, but it had no garden. So she loved to walk through the meadows just to look at the flowers. Princess Sylvie loved flowers!

One day Princess Sylvie found an overgrown path. She asked a woman where the path led.

"That path leads to the garden of the enchantress!" said the woman.

"What is an enchantress?" Princess Sylvie asked.

"Someone who uses magic! So be warned... don't pick the flowers, or who knows what terrible things might happen!"

Princess Sylvie followed the path until she came to a small cottage with the prettiest garden she had ever seen. It was filled with flowers of every colour and perfume!

After that, Princess Sylvie went every day. Winter came and snow lay thick, yet the garden stayed the same.

Princess Sylvie forgot all about the enchantress. One wintry day, she picked a rose from the garden and took it back to the castle. As she put it in water, Princess Sylvie suddenly remembered the warning. She'd picked a flower from the enchanted garden, and who knew what terrible things might happen?

But days passed and nothing happened. The rose stayed as fresh as the day it was picked.

Then months passed and still nothing happened. Forgetting her fears, Princess Sylvie decided to go back to the enchanted garden.

When she saw the garden, Princess Sylvie wanted to cry. The grass was brown. The flowers had withered and died. Then she heard someone weeping.

Inside the cottage the enchantress was sitting by the fire, crying. She was old and bent. Although Princess Sylvie was afraid, she felt sorry for her.

"What happened to your garden?" Princess Sylvie asked.

"Someone picked a rose from my magic garden!" said the enchantress. "The rose will live for ever, but the rest must die!"

"Can't your magic bring the garden back to life?" Princess Sylvie asked.

"Alas, when the rose was picked, my magic was lost. And now, I too will wither and die."

"What can I do?" asked Princess Sylvie, heartbroken.

"Only a princess can bring my magic back," she replied.

"How?" asked Princess Sylvie.

"She must bring me six sacks full of stinging nettles. No princess would do such a thing."

Princess Sylvie didn't say anything. She turned and ran to the meadow. She gathered up armful after armful of nettles, not caring that they stung her. She filled six sacks and took them back to the enchantress.

"You are kind," she said. "But the nettles must be picked by a princess."

"But I am a princess," said Princess Sylvie.

Without delay, the enchantress made a magic potion with the nettles and drank it. Instantly, the garden became enchanted again! Princess Sylvie gasped. Gone was the bent old lady and in her place was a young woman.

"My beautiful garden is restored," smiled the enchantress, "and so am I!"

And so the enchantress and the princess became great friends and shared the enchanted garden.

Cinderella

Once upon a time, there lived a very pretty little girl. When she was young, sadly, her mother died. Her father remarried, but the girl's stepmother was a mean woman with two ugly daughters.

These stepsisters were so jealous of the young girl's beauty that they treated her like a servant and made her sit among the cinders in the kitchen.

They called her Cinderella, and before long everyone, even her father, had forgotten the little girl's real name.

Cinderella missed her real mother more and more each day.

One day, an invitation arrived from the royal palace. The king and queen were holding a ball for the prince's twenty-first birthday, and all the fine ladies of the kingdom were invited.

Cinderella's stepsisters were very excited when their invitations arrived.

"I will wear my red velvet gown!" cried the first stepsister. "And the black pearl necklace that Mother gave to me."

"And I will wear my blue silk dress!" cried the other. "With a silver tiara."

"Come, Cinderella!" they called. "You must help us to get ready!"

Cinderella helped her stepsisters with their silk stockings and frilly petticoats. She brushed and curled their hair and powdered their cheeks and noses. At last, she squeezed them into their beautiful ball gowns.

But even after all this, the two ugly stepsisters weren't nearly as lovely as Cinderella was in her rags. This made them both very jealous and very angry, and they began to tease her.

"Too bad you can't come to the ball, Cinders!" sneered the first stepsister.

"Yes," laughed the other one. "They'd never let a shabby creature like you near the palace!"

Cinderella said nothing, but inside her heart was breaking. She really wanted to go to the ball.

After her stepsisters left, she sat and wept.

"Dry your tears, my dear," said a gentle voice.

Cinderella was amazed. A kind old woman stood before her. In her hand was a sparkly wand that shone.

"I am your Fairy Godmother," she told Cinderella. "And you shall go to the ball!"

"But I have nothing to wear! And how will I get there?" cried Cinderella.

The Fairy Godmother smiled!

She asked Cinders to fetch her the biggest pumpkin in the garden. With a flick of her magic wand she turned it into a golden carriage, and the mice in the kitchen mousetrap into fine horses.

A fat rat soon became a handsome coachman.

Cinderella couldn't believe her eyes.

Smiling, the Fairy Godmother waved her wand once more and suddenly Cinders was dressed in a splendid ball gown, with sparkling glass slippers on her feet.

"My magic ends at midnight, so you must be home before then," said the Fairy Godmother.

When Cinderella arrived at the ball, everyone was dazzled by her beauty. Whispers went round the ballroom as the other guests wondered who this enchanting stranger could be. Even Cinderella's own stepsisters did not recognise her.

As soon as the prince saw Cinderella, he fell in love with her. "Would you do me the honour of this dance?" he asked.

"Why certainly, sir," Cinderella answered. And from that moment on he only had eyes for Cinderella.

Soon the clock struck midnight. "I must go!" said Cinderella, suddenly remembering her promise to her Fairy Godmother.

She fled from the ballroom and ran down the palace steps. The prince ran after her, but when he got outside, she was gone. He didn't notice a grubby servant girl holding a pumpkin. A few mice and a rat were scurrying around her feet.

But there on the steps was one dainty glass slipper. The prince picked it up and rushed back into the palace. "Does anyone know who this slipper belongs to?" he cried.

The next day, Cinderella's stepsisters could talk of nothing but the ball, and the beautiful stranger who had danced all night with the prince. As they were talking, there was a knock at the door.

"Cinderella, quick, jump to it and see who it is," called her stepmother. Standing on the doorstep was His Highness the Prince with one of the royal footmen, who was holding the little glass slipper on a velvet cushion.

"The lady whose foot this slipper fits is my one and only true love," said the prince. "I am visiting every house in the kingdom in search of her."

The two stepsisters began shoving each other out of the way in their rush to try on the slipper. They both squeezed and pushed as hard as they could, but their clumsy feet were far too big for the tiny glass shoe.

Then Cinderella stepped forward. "Please, Your Highness," she said shyly, "may I try?"

As her stepsisters watched in utter amazement, Cinderella slid her foot into the dainty slipper. It fitted as if it were made for her!

As the prince gazed into her eyes, he knew he had found his love – and Cinderella knew she had found hers.

Cinderella and the prince soon set a date to be married.

On the day of their wedding, the land rang with the sound of bells, and the sun shone as the people cheered. Even Cinderella's nasty stepsisters were invited. Everyone had a really wonderful day, and Cinderella and her prince lived happily ever after.

Puss in Boots

There was once a miller who had three sons.
When he died, he left his mill to the eldest son,
his cottage to his middle son and only his pet cat
to his youngest son, William.

William went and sat under a tree, feeling
very miserable and sorry for himself. "What will
become of us, Puss?" he moaned.

To William's utter amazement, Puss
answered him.

"Don't worry, master," said the cat. "Just do
what I say and you will be far richer than either
of your brothers!"

Puss told William to get him a fine suit of clothes, a pair of soft leather boots and a strong canvas sack. Then he caught a huge rabbit, put it in the sack, and took it to the palace.

No one there had ever seen a talking cat before, so he was granted an immediate audience with the king.

"Your Majesty," said Puss, "this fine rabbit is a gift from my master, the Marquis of Carabas."

The king had never heard of the Marquis of Carabas, but he was too embarrassed to admit this. "Please thank the Marquis," he said to Puss, "and give him my regards."

The next day, Puss caught some plump partridges and once more he took them to the king, with the same message: "These are from my master."

For several months, Puss went on bringing the king fine gifts.

One day, he heard that the king would be riding along the river bank that afternoon with the princess.

"Master," said Puss, "you must go swimming in the river today."

"Why?" asked William.

"Just do as I say, and you will see," answered Puss.

While William was swimming, Puss hid all his clothes. Then, when he saw the king's carriage approaching, he ran up to it shouting for help.

"Help!" cried Puss. "Robbers have stolen my master's clothes!"

When the king recognised the cat, he called to his chief steward and ordered him to bring a fine new suit from the palace.

"It must be of the finest cut," said the king, "and made from the softest cloth, you hear! Only the best will do for the Marquis of Carabas!"

Once he was dressed in his fine new suit, William looked quite handsome. The princess invited him to join her and her father in the carriage.

As William and the princess sat side by side, they began to fall in love.

Meanwhile, Puss ran ahead until he came to a meadow where he saw some men mowing. "The king's carriage is coming," Puss told them. "When he asks whose meadow this is, say it belongs to the Marquis of Carabas – or you will have your heads cut off!"

The mowers didn't dare to disobey.

When the royal carriage came by, the king asked who the meadow belonged to. The mowers quickly replied, "The Marquis of Carabas."

"I can see that you are very well off indeed," the king said to William, who blushed modestly. That made the princess love him even more!

Down the road, Puss came to a field where men were harvesting corn. "When the king asks whose corn this is," Puss told them, "say it belongs to the Marquis of Carabas – or you will have your heads cut off!"

The harvesters didn't dare to disobey.

Next, Puss came to an enormous castle which he knew belonged to a fierce ogre. Still he bravely knocked on the door.

When the ogre let him in, Puss bowed low and said, "I have heard that you have wondrous powers and can change yourself into anything – even a lion or an elephant."

"That is true," said the ogre. And to prove it, he changed himself into a snarling, growling lion.

Puss was terrified and leapt up onto a cupboard. Then the ogre changed himself back again.

"That was amazing," Puss remarked. "But surely it cannot be too difficult for someone of your size to change into a creature as big as a lion. If you were truly the magician they say you are, you could turn into something tiny – like a mouse."

"Of course I can do that!" bellowed the ogre. In an instant he became a little brown mouse scurrying across the floor.

Quick as a flash, Puss leapt off the cupboard, pounced on the mouse and ate it in one big gulp!

Soon, Puss heard the king's carriage drawing near and rushed outside. As it approached, he bowed low and said, "Welcome, Your Majesty, to the home of the Marquis of Carabas."

The king was very impressed indeed. "May we come in?" he asked William.

"Of course, Your Majesty," replied William, a little confused.

As they walked through the castle, the king was delighted to see treasures of great value everywhere he looked. He was so pleased that he said to William, "You are the perfect husband for my daughter."

William and the princess were very happy and later that day they were married. They lived in the ogre's castle happily ever after. Puss, of course, lived with them – though he never chased mice again!

Sleeping Beauty

Once upon a time, in a land far, far away, there lived a king and queen who were kind and good. When the queen gave birth to a baby girl, the whole kingdom rejoiced.

When it was time for the baby to be christened, the king and queen arranged a great celebration. They asked the seven good fairies of the kingdom to be the baby's godmothers. But eight fairies arrived at the feast.

The eighth fairy was ugly and old, and no one had seen her for years. The king and queen, thinking she was dead, hadn't invited her to take part in the ceremony.

Soon it was time for the fairies to give the baby princess their magical presents. The first gave her the gift of beauty, the second gave her wisdom. The third fairy said she would be graceful, the fourth said that she would dance like the wind. The fifth and sixth gave her the gift of music and song, so that she would sing and play like an angel.

Just before the seventh fairy stepped up to give the princess her gift, the eighth fairy pushed in front of her.

"On her sixteenth birthday," she cackled, "the princess will prick her finger on the spindle of a spinning wheel – and she will die!"

Everyone in the room was horrified, and the queen began to cry. But then the seventh fairy stepped forwards. "Here is my gift," she said. "The princess will not die. Instead, when she pricks her finger, she will fall asleep for a hundred years. At the end of that time, a prince will come to wake her up."

The king and queen were relieved, but even so they ordered every spinning wheel in the kingdom to be destroyed. They couldn't bear to think of anything hurting their daughter.

The years passed and the princess grew into a lovely young girl, as wise, beautiful and graceful as the fairies had promised.

On the day of her sixteenth birthday, she was wandering through the castle when she came to a small room in a tall tower. Inside, an old woman sat spinning thread.

"My dear," cackled the old woman, "come here and try this for yourself."

As soon as the princess's hand touched the spindle, she pricked her finger and fell to the floor in a deep sleep.

When they discovered their daughter, the king and queen were heartbroken, for they knew that she would not wake for a hundred years. They called for the palace guard, who gently laid the sleeping princess on a golden stretcher and carried her to the royal bedchamber. There they placed her on a bed with silken pillows and velvet covers. The king and queen watched over her and cried.

"Oh, my dear," said the queen to her husband. "How are we ever going to cope without our darling daughter?"

The fairy who had saved the princess's life heard what had happened. Worried that the princess would wake up in a world where she knew no one, she cast a spell over the whole castle. Everyone, from the guards and the kitchen maids to the gardeners and the cooks – even the princess's pet dog – fell into a deep, deep sleep.

Then the fairy made tall trees and twisting, sharp brambles grow around the castle, surrounding it with a thick thorny wall that no one could get through.

Only the very tops of the castle's towers could be seen.
And so a hundred years went by.

One day, a prince from a nearby land was out riding
when he saw the tops of the castle
towers rising from the
middle of the thick,
dark wood. He
asked some of
the country
people about the
castle, and they
told him the
story of the
Sleeping
Beauty.
"Many
people have
wanted to
get through
those
thorns,"
they told
him, "but
they have all
died trying."

The prince was determined to be the one who succeeded and set off towards the mysterious castle.

To the prince's amazement, the thorny brambles and the twisting branches of the dark trees let him pass through easily. He reached the castle door, and went inside.

The prince walked through many halls and chambers where people and animals slept as if they were dead. He searched every room and chamber, until he found the very one where the beautiful princess slept.

"Oh, princess!" cried the prince. "You are more beautiful than the most delicate rose ever found."

The prince moved quietly towards the sleeping princess and gazed down lovingly at her. He gently took her tiny hand in his, and as love filled his heart, he knelt beside her and slowly kissed her red lips. Instantly the princess's eyes opened.

"Is it you, my prince?" she said, when she saw him. "I have waited such a long time for you!"

At that moment the spell was broken, and everyone else in the castle woke up, too.

That evening, the princess's sixteenth birthday was celebrated with a joyous party – a hundred years too late!

The princess and her prince danced together all evening, and soon after, they were married. They lived together in happiness for many, many years.

Rapunzel

Once upon a time there lived a couple who, after many years, found they were expecting a baby.

Their tiny cottage stood next to a river. Across the river was a beautiful garden full of glorious flowers and tasty-looking vegetables.

One day, the woman looked across the river and saw a vegetable called rampion growing in the garden. It looked delicious, and she longed to taste it. She begged her husband to get some for her.

The garden belonged to an evil witch, and the husband refused. But his wife would eat nothing else, and grew thin and pale.

At last he agreed, so that night, the man crossed the river and picked handfuls of rampion from the witch's garden.

Suddenly the evil witch appeared. "How dare you steal from me!" she roared.

"F-forgive me," the man stammered. "My wife is expecting a baby and longed for some of this vegetable. If she doesn't have it, I'm afraid that she will die."

"Very well," said the witch, "take all you want. But you must give me something in return. When your baby is born, I must have it."

Terrified, the man agreed and fled.

67

The wife was overjoyed and made a salad with the rampion. She ate it hungrily.

After that, the man went to the witch's garden every day. He brought home baskets of rampion, and his wife grew strong and healthy. A few months later she gave birth to a beautiful baby girl.

The man had forgotten all about his promise to the witch, but when the baby was just a day old, the witch burst in and took her away. The baby's parents were heartbroken and never saw her or the witch again.

The witch called the baby Rapunzel. She took her to a cottage deep in a forest, and took good care of her.

68

On Rapunzel's twelfth birthday, the cruel witch imprisoned her in a forbidding high tower, with no doors and just one small window at the very top.

Every day the witch came and stood at the bottom of the tower, and called, "Rapunzel, Rapunzel! Let down your long hair!" Rapunzel would let down her long, golden hair, and the witch would begin to climb up.

Rapunzel spent many lonely years in her tower. To pass the time, she often sat by the window and sang.

One day, a prince rode through the forest. Enchanted by the sound of Rapunzel's sweet voice, the young prince followed it until he came to the doorless tower.

Just then the witch arrived. The prince quickly hid as she called: "Rapunzel, Rapunzel! Let down your long hair!"

The witch climbed up the hair, and the prince knew that this was the way he would be able to meet the owner of the beautiful voice. After the witch had gone, the prince stood beneath the tower and called out in a voice like the witch's, "Rapunzel, Rapunzel! Let down your long hair!"

When Rapunzel's golden hair came tumbling down, he climbed up to the window.

70

Rapunzel was frightened when she saw the prince. But he was gentle and kind, and she quickly lost her fear. The prince came to see Rapunzel often, and they soon fell in love. He asked her to marry him – but how would Rapunzel leave the tower?

Rapunzel had an idea. "Each time you visit," she told the prince, "bring me a ball of strong silk. I will plait it into a long, long ladder. When it is finished I will climb down and run away to marry you."

The prince did as Rapunzel asked, and soon the ladder was ready.

But on the very day she was to run away, something terrible happened. When the witch climbed through the window, Rapunzel absent-mindedly said, "Why do you pull so hard at my hair? The prince is not so rough." Suddenly, Rapunzel realised what she had said.

71

The witch flew into a raging fury. "You ungrateful little wretch!" she screamed. "I have protected you from the world, and you have betrayed me. Now you must be punished!"

"I'm sorry," Rapunzel sobbed, as she fell to her knees. "I didn't mean to make you cross."

The witch grabbed a pair of scissors and – snip-snap-snip-snap – cut off Rapunzel's long golden hair. Then, using the ladder to climb down, the witch carried Rapunzel off to a faraway land, where she left her to wander all alone without any food, water or anything to keep her warm.

That evening, when the prince called, the witch let down Rapunzel's hair. The prince climbed quickly up, and couldn't believe his eyes!

"The bird has flown, my pretty!" the witch cackled evilly. "You will never see Rapunzel again!"

Overcome with grief, the sad prince threw himself from the tower. His fall was broken by some brambles, but they also scratched and blinded him.

The prince stumbled away and wandered the land for a year, living on berries and rainwater.

Then one day the prince heard a beautiful sound – the sweet voice of Rapunzel! He called her name and she ran into his arms, weeping tears of joy. The tears fell onto the prince's wounded eyes and suddenly he could see again.

The prince took Rapunzel home to his castle, where they were married and lived happily ever after.

The Pink Princess

Princess Sophia loved pink.
She had a bright pink room... with a plump pink bed.
She had a huge pink wardrobe full of frilly pink dresses.
She had rosebud pink shoes... and a pink tiara.

One day, Princess Chloe came to play at the palace for the very first time. She brought Pink Princess Sophia a lovely new necklace! But there was only one problem...

"It's not pink!"cried Princess Sophia.

"This is a very kind gift," said the king.

"Look how it sparkles in the sun," said the queen.

Princess Sophia peered at the necklace. It really was beautiful. But it wouldn't go with her pink dress, pink shoes, or pink tiara!

"Come on, Princess Sophia," said Princess Chloe. "Let's go and play!"

Princess Sophia put the necklace in her pocket, and, with a nod from the king and queen, she followed Princess Chloe into the palace gardens.

Princess Chloe picked a beautiful red flower. Princess Sophia looked at her in surprise. "Are you sure we're allowed to pick flowers?" she said.

"Why not?" said Princess Chloe. "Look, here's a pink one, too!"

And she skipped away, through the garden, picking differently coloured flowers for her hair as she went. Princess Sophia looked at the pink flower, but then she noticed some bright purple blossoms.

She picked some of the blossoms and put them in her hair, just like Princess Chloe.

Princess Chloe started to climb a huge tree. Princess Sophia couldn't believe her eyes!

"Princesses don't climb trees!" she gasped.

"Why not?" said Princess Chloe. "Look, I've found some ribbons up here!"

Princess Sophia recognised the ribbons of a kite she had lost, streaming like a rainbow in the breeze. She climbed up into the tree and felt like a bird among the bright green leaves.

Princess Chloe untangled the ribbons and tied one around her waist.

She tied one for Princess Sophia, too.

"Now catch me if you can!" said Princess Chloe. She scrambled down the tree, and Princess Sophia followed closely behind. Princess Sophia giggled as leaves caught in her hair.

Princess Chloe ran to the meadow.

"Look, ladybirds!" she said, kneeling down to see them.

"Princesses shouldn't crawl about getting dirty!" said Princess Sophia.

"How else can you see all these amazing creatures?" asked Princess Chloe.

Princess Sophia knelt down beside her.

"Look," she said. "There goes a grasshopper, too!"

Something pink glinted between the trees.

"Let's explore over there!" said Princess Chloe. They ran to fallen petals floating on a lily pond.

Princess Chloe dabbled her fingers in the water.

"I suppose princesses can get wet, too?" laughed Princess Sophia.

"I'm making friends with the fishes," said Princess Chloe.

A dragonfly fluttered
over the pond, its colourful
wings catching the sun.

Princess Chloe whispered to the dragonfly,
"She doesn't like anything that isn't pink."
The dragonfly's wings drooped. It landed on
Princess Chloe's outstretched hand. Princess
Sophia jumped back nervously.

"Yes, I do!" shouted Princess Sophia. "I like the bright flowers and the green leaves, and the blue pond and this shimmering dragonfly with the most gorgeous, most colourful wings I have ever seen!"

The dragonfly stretched out its wings proudly.

"Why don't you try on your new necklace now?" asked Princess Chloe. She helped Princess Sophia fasten the delicate clasp.

Princess Sophia admired her colourful reflection in the pond. Then she smiled.

"I don't mind that it's not a pink necklace..." she said. "Because I'm not just a pink princess any more!"

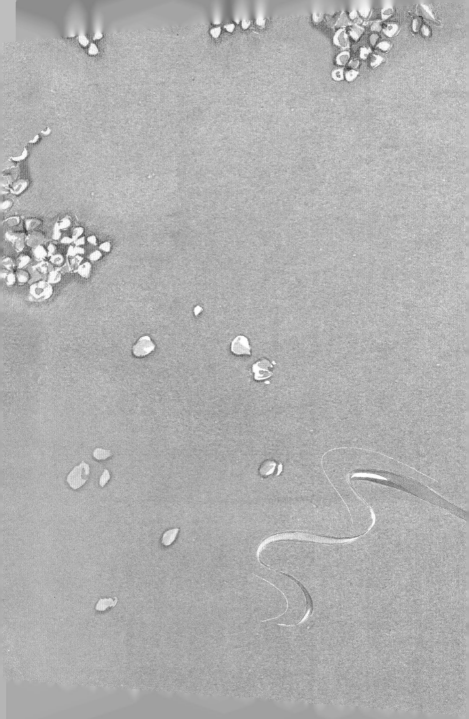